The Hungry Little Monkey

by Andy Blackford

Illustrated by Gabriele Antonini

FRANKLIN WATTS
LONDON•SYDNEY

Notes on the series

TIDDLERS are structured to provide support for children who are starting to read on their own. The stories may also be used for sharing with children.

Starting to read alone can be daunting. **TIDDLERS** help by listing the words in the book for a check before reading, and by providing visual support and repeating words and phrases. These books will both develop confidence and encourage reading and rereading for pleasure.

If you are reading this book with a child, here are a few suggestions:

1. Make reading fun! Choose a time to read when you and the child are relaxed and have time to share the story.
2. Talk about the story before you start reading. Look at the cover and the blurb. What might the story be about? Why might the child like it?
3. Look also at the list of words below - can the child tackle most of the words?
4. Encourage the child to retell the story, using the jumbled picture puzzle.
5. Give praise! Remember that small mistakes need not always be corrected.

Here is a list of the words in this story.

Common words:

a	it	said
asked	little	that
at	looked	was
for	mum	
he	not	

Other words:

banana	monkey	squeeze
bite	parrot	suck
did	peck	tiger
hungry	peel	work
lion	snake	yum

Little Monkey
was hungry.

He asked for a banana.

He looked at it.

"Bite it!" said Tiger.

That did not work.

"Peck it!" said Parrot.

11

That did not work.

"Suck it!" said Lion.

14

16

"Squeeze it!" said Snake.

That did not work.

"Peel it!" said Mum.

20

"Yum!" said Little Monkey.

Puzzle Time

Can you find these
pictures in the story?

Which pages are the pictures from?

Turn over for answers!

Answers

The pictures come from these pages:

a. pages 12 and 13

b. pages 6 and 7

c. pages 16 and 17

d. pages 10 and 11

First published in 2010 by
Franklin Watts
338 Euston Road
London
NW1 3BH

Franklin Watts Australia
Level 17/207 Kent Street
Sydney
NSW 2000

Text © Andy Blackford 2010
Illustration © Gabriele Antonini 2010

The rights of Andy Blackford to be
identified as the author and Gabriele
Antonini as the illustrator of this Work
have been asserted in accordance with the
Copyright, Designs and Patents Act, 1988.

A CIP catalogue record for this book is
available from the British Library.

ISBN 978 0 7496 9390 9 (hbk)
ISBN 978 0 7496 9402 9 (pbk)

Series Editor: Jackie Hamley
Editor: Melanie Palmer
Series Advisor: Catherine Glavina
Series Designer: Peter Scoulding

Printed in China

Franklin Watts is a division of Hachette Children's Books,
an Hachette UK company. www.hachette.co.uk